Allie's Rabbit

Helen Dunmore

Illustrated by Simone Lia

For Tess
H.D.

For my sister Mirielle
S.L.

First published in Great Britain in 1999
by Mammoth, an imprint of Egmont Children's Books Limited
239 Kensington High Street, London, W8 6SA

Text copyright © 1999 Helen Dunmore
Illustrations copyright © 1999 Simone Lia

The moral rights of the author and illustrator have been asserted

The rights of Helen Dunmore and Simone Lia to be identified as
the author and illustrator of this work have been asserted by them
in accordance with the Copyright, Designs and Patents Act 1988
ISBN 0 7497 3530 9

10 9 8 7 6 5 4 3 2 1

A CIP catalogue record for this book
is available from the British Library

Printed in Great Britain by Cox & Wyman Ltd,
Reading, Berkshire

Contents

~

1

Allie's rabbit

19

Misha's swimming lesson

37

The big snow

56

The best party ever

1

Allie's rabbit

'That one,' said Misha, pointing. 'That's the one I'd buy.'

Allie looked. It was a soft, small, white rabbit, scuffling down in a heap of wood shavings. As if he'd heard Misha's voice, he turned round and looked at them. His nose quivered. 'Oh, look at his eyes! They're all pink!' said Allie.

'I know. I think they're beautiful,' said Misha.

Allie said nothing, but she didn't really like the pink eyes. The rabbit Allie wanted had dark brown eyes, shiny as toffees. All the rabbits in this pen were male. Her rabbit looked at Allie as if he already knew who she was. He had soft fur which was a mixture of brown and grey and silver. Allie longed to touch him. She leaned over the barrier, but she couldn't quite reach.

Suddenly one of the boys who worked at Pets' World on Saturdays swung his legs over the barrier, bent down and picked up Allie's rabbit. He lifted the rabbit high in the air and called to a man standing by the till, 'Was this the one you wanted?'

Allie and Misha looked at each other. 'That's my rabbit,' whispered Allie.

'I know,' said Misha. They waited. The man by the till strolled up to the pen and peered at Allie's rabbit.

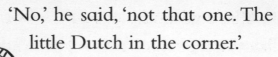

'No,' he said, 'not that one. The little Dutch in the corner.'

Allie's breath came out in a rush. She grabbed tight on to Misha's hand.

'You've got to buy him quick, before someone else gets him,' said Misha.

'I know, but Mum won't let me.'

'Did you ask her again this morning?'

Allie nodded. 'I even showed her all the money I've saved up. And I told her I'd have the rabbit hutch for Christmas as well as my birthday.'

'But she still said no?'

'She said I wouldn't know how to look after it properly.'

Misha looked at Allie. It was a long, clear look. It made Allie wonder if she really would be able to look after a pet properly.

'I'm sure you would,' said Misha. Allie smiled at her. Suddenly she felt quite sure that somehow, some day soon, she was going to get her rabbit. She could almost see herself filling his food bowl, washing out his water bottle, clipping his nails, stroking his floppy ears.

'You mustn't give up,' said Misha.

'It's Jacqueline as well,' said Allie. 'She says *she's* never had a pet, so it's not fair if I have a rabbit.'

'Does she want one?'

'No.'

'She just doesn't want *you* to have one, then,' said Misha.

'I know,' said Allie sadly. She watched her rabbit digging deep into the hay. He thought he was digging a tunnel, but he wasn't really.

'Look at him, he thinks he's hiding,' she said to Misha. 'He's so sweet. I wish I could have him.'

At tea-time Mum came home with a shiny, pleased face and a box of chocolate whirl cakes. 'I've had a tax rebate in my pay this month!' she said.

'What's that?' asked Allie.

'Money,' said Mum. 'And it's come at just the right time. I'm going to decorate your bedroom. You can have new duvet covers as well. We'll have to think about colours.'

'Red,' said Allie.

'Yellow,' said Jacqueline. 'Yellow walls, white ceiling, yellow-and-white duvet covers and two big yellow cushions on each of our beds.'

Allie could see their bedroom as if it had already been decorated. Yellow and white without a spot of red in it anywhere. Jacqueline was even telling Mum where to buy the duvet covers. It didn't matter what Allie said, Jacqueline would get her way.

Allie said nothing while Jacqueline talked on and on about the yellow and white bedroom. She didn't leave any space for Allie to argue. After a while Mum and Jacqueline looked at her.

'You're very quiet, Allie,' said Mum.

'She likes yellow, don't you, Allie?' said Jacqueline.

'No,' said Allie. 'I like red.'

'Red!' shouted Jacqueline. 'I don't believe it! Red!'

'Oh dear,' said Mum. 'I was afraid of this.' She didn't look shiny and pleased any more. She looked tired.

'But our bedroom can be yellow if Jacqueline wants,' said Allie. Jacqueline stared at Allie with her mouth open. 'If –'

'If what?' asked Mum sharply.

'If I can have a rabbit,' said Allie quickly, not looking at Mum. 'I've saved up loads of money and I'll pay for his food and his hay and everything, and I'll have the hutch for my birthday and Christmas present.'

Mum lay back in her chair. 'Oh, Allie,' she said. She shut her eyes. 'I'm not having you and Jacqueline quarrelling all the time about a rabbit.'

Jacqueline fixed her eyes on Allie. She looked like next door's cat watching a bird. 'Do you really mean it, Allie?' she asked. 'You really mean I can choose the colours for our bedroom?'

'Yes,' said Allie.

'Yellow and white? No red?'

'No red,' said Allie.

'Mum,' said Jacqueline, 'I don't mind if Allie has a rabbit.'

Allie held Silver in her arms. She could feel his heart beating and the tickle of his soft, greyish-silver fur under her chin. He was the most beautiful rabbit Allie had ever seen. Misha was kneeling on the floor, putting layers of newspaper into the new hutch.

'And then the wood shavings, and the hay goes in here,' said Misha. 'They need loads of hay in winter, to keep them warm.'

'How do you know?' asked Allie.

'I read a book,' Misha said. She gave Allie her quick little smile. Allie decided that Silver was going to be the best-looked-after rabbit in the world. Clean water every day. Fresh food morning and evening. Loads of hay and wood shavings. She was going to clean out the whole hutch every week and scrub it with disinfectant.

'It's fantastic, having a rabbit,' said Allie.

'I know,' said Misha.

'You can sort of share Silver, if you want.'

'No,' said Misha, 'you can't really share a rabbit. He's yours.'

Silver loved dandelion leaves. Every time Misha and Allie went to the park they picked dandelion leaves for him.

Sometimes Mrs Patel at the corner shop gave Allie cabbages which were too old to sell. Everybody knew about Silver.

Once Allie gave him lettuce, but it made him ill. Allie had to clean out the whole hutch in the middle of the week, and it took ages. There wasn't time to go round and watch Misha's new video.

'I don't mind, Silver,' Allie whispered, and she stroked his ears. He jumped out of her arms and raced round and round the back yard so fast that Allie couldn't catch him.

'Silver! There's Spangles on the wall! He'll eat you if he catches you.'

But Silver didn't know cats were dangerous. When Allie caught him, he scratched her arm and left a long red mark.

'Silver!' said Allie.

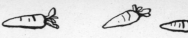

'I'm trying to save your life and all you do is scratch me.'

Silver was so beautiful. Every day Allie rushed home from school so she could play with him. He liked carrots, but not apples. He wasn't afraid of Spangles, but when Allie brought her old toy dog into the back yard Silver hid right at the back of his hutch.

'You're so silly, Silver,' Allie said.

Suddenly the days got darker. It was nearly dark when Allie got home from school. There was only just time to change Silver's water bottle and give him his food. Allie didn't have time to clean out his bowl every day. Allie wished she could bring him inside, but she knew Mum would never let her.

'See you in the morning, Silver!' she said, and ran indoors.

The nights grew colder.

'Put a blanket over his hutch at night,'

said Misha, 'and turn his hutch round to face the wall. That'll keep him warm.'

'Is that in the book as well?' asked Allie.

'Yes,' said Misha.

'I'll do it every single night,' said Allie.

Mum had an old baby blanket that used to be Allie's. Allie folded it over and tucked it round the hutch so it looked warm and cosy. Then she shivered and ran inside.

It grew darker and colder every night. Sometimes there was frost on the ground. One night, when Allie went to get some more hay out of the bag, she found it was nearly empty.

I must ask Mum to take me to Pets' World tomorrow, she thought. But the next day Allie stayed on after school for gym club, and she forgot about the hay.

Never mind, I'll get some tomorrow. I'll tuck his blanket right over the hutch to keep him warm. But when Allie looked in the back yard, she couldn't find Silver's blanket. It wasn't on the hutch. It wasn't tucked into the hay bag. Allie burst into the kitchen.

'Mum, have you seen Silver's blanket?'

'Oh, Allie, Spangles was dragging it round the yard. It was filthy, so I put it in the washing-machine. It's on the radiator. It'll be dry later on.'

'Mum! He needs it! It's freezing.'

'Allie, Silver's got plenty of hay. He'll be fine.'

Allie didn't want to tell Mum about the empty hay bag. Anyway, it didn't matter. Later on she was going to take the warm blanket out and put it over the hutch. She wasn't going to let Silver catch cold.

It was a cold, cold night. So cold that Allie burrowed deep down under her yellow-and-white duvet. Soon she grew warm and drowsy. Jacqueline was still downstairs finishing her homework when Allie drifted into sleep.

Allie woke in the deep middle of the night. Her duvet had fallen off and she was freezing. For a minute she thought she was outside. Then she remembered Silver.

'Oh no!' A shock of fear went through her and she felt suddenly hot. She hadn't put Silver's blanket on. She hadn't turned his hutch round. She hadn't made sure there was hay in the bag. She hadn't looked after him at all. Silver was out in the icy yard.

'Freezing!' said Allie. She sat up, lifted the corner of the curtain, and peeped out. It was dark and there were strange streetlamp shadows. It was very quiet and very still. There was nothing moving at all.

'Oh no! Silver!' Allie jumped out of bed. She didn't dare put on the kitchen light in case she woke Mum. She peered through the glass in the back door, but she couldn't see the hutch. There was no sound. The yard was crowded with shadows. Allie took a deep breath. She was afraid of the dark yard. Maybe Silver would be all right. After all, he had lots of fur to keep him warm. Then, suddenly, Allie thought of Misha. Misha was so sure that Allie could look after a rabbit properly. Allie remembered how Misha had read the rabbit book and helped her to get the hutch ready for Silver. Slowly, slowly, Allie stretched out her hand and slid back the bolt on the door. Then she turned the key, and opened the back door. The night frost stung through her pyjamas as she stepped into the yard.

It was so dark she could hardly see the hutch, even when she was right beside it. Allie put out her hand and felt for the mesh of wire on the front of the hutch. But her hand touched soft wool. Soft, thick wool. Like a blanket. It *was* a blanket. Silver's blanket was tucked over the hutch. And the hutch was turned to the wall, away from the cold. Allie kneeled down and listened. Inside the hutch she heard a sleepy scuffling.

'I'm sorry, Silver,' she whispered. 'You'll

have lots of hay tomorrow, I promise. I'm sorry I forgot you.'

And then a shadow moved.

'Argh!' said Allie.

'Shut up, Allie. It's only me.'

'Jacqueline!'

'I heard you go downstairs.'

'I was worried about Silver,' said Allie. 'I forgot his blanket, but Mum must have put it on.'

'No,' said Jacqueline. 'It was me. And I turned his hutch round. I saw you'd forgotten.'

Allie did not know what to say.

'I'm freezing,' said Jacqueline. 'Let's go back to bed.'

Allie's feet were like cold stones. She curled up under her duvet, rubbing her feet together. She was sure that in the other bed, under the yellow-and-white duvet, Jacqueline was still awake. The darkness seemed to be listening and waiting for something.

'Thank you, Jacqueline,' whispered Allie. 'Listen. If you want, you can sort of share Silver with me.'

Allie held her breath to hear what Jacqueline would say. She waited and waited, but there was no answer. Maybe Jacqueline was already asleep.

2

Misha's swimming lesson

'Next week we have our first swimming session, on Tuesday morning,' said Mrs Button. She had a pile of notes in her hand. 'These notes are for you to take home.'

'Swimming!' said Allie. 'That's fantastic! Swimming all morning instead of school!' She took her note from Mrs Button.

'Now remember, Allie, give

this to your mother as soon as you get home. Don't leave it in the bottom of your schoolbag again.'

Allie often left notes in the bottom of her schoolbag. But this time she wouldn't forget. 'I'll give it to Mum as soon as she gets back from work, I promise!' she told Mrs Button.

Then it was playtime. Allie and Misha shared Misha's KitKat.

'I can't wait for next Tuesday, can you?' asked Allie. Misha didn't answer. Maybe it was because her mouth was full of KitKat. 'Swimming!' said Allie. 'You remember what Mrs Button said? Our class is going swimming.'

'I know,' said Misha. Allie looked at her. Misha's face was still and serious.

'Don't you want to go?' asked Allie. 'Don't you like swimming?'

'I don't know,' said Misha. 'I've never been to a swimming-pool.'

Never been to a swimming-pool! Allie nearly shouted it out loud she was so surprised, but she just managed to say nothing.

Allie had started going to the swimming-pool when she was two. She couldn't remember not being able to swim. First of all swimming with little red armbands with yellow ducks on them, then doggy-paddle, then breast-stroke, like Mum. Allie could swim underwater, and she could dive off the side of the pool. She could nearly do an underwater somersault, but the water kept going up her nose. Allie thought the swimming-pool was the best place in the world. And Misha had never been there.

'Doesn't your mum ever take you?' asked Allie.

'No,' said Misha. 'Well, you know, she's busy with Vivi.'

Allie nodded. Vivi was only a baby. But Allie had seen lots of babies in the swimming-pool, with tiny baby armbands on, splashing and laughing. And, anyway, why couldn't Misha's dad take her? Allie looked at Misha again.

'Let's have a race!' said Misha quickly. 'First one to the climbing-frame!'

Allie's swimsuit was too small. When she tried it on, the straps dug into her shoulders, and Mum said, 'Oh dear, Allie, we're going to have to get another. Let me see. We'll go on Saturday afternoon, and we'll get you some new goggles as well.'

'Can Misha come?' asked Allie.

'Yes, all right.'

'Misha can get her swimsuit, too,' said Allie.

The sports shop had rows of swimsuits. Allie knew which one she wanted straight away. Dark blue, with a white logo on the front. Mum riffled through the row of swimsuits until she found the right size, then she gave it to Allie and said, 'Go and try it on. What about you, Misha? Which one do you like?'

But Misha wasn't sure.

'Try one like mine,' said Allie, but Misha shook her head.

'Red would look nice on you,' said Mum. 'What about this one?'

Misha took the red swimsuit, and gave Mum her money to look after. Allie and Misha went to try on the swimsuits. It took Allie ages to get hers on because there was a label tangled round the straps. When she came out of the cubicle Misha was standing in front of the mirror in the red swimsuit.

'Does it fit you?' asked Allie.

'I think so,' said Misha. She stared at her reflection. 'But I can't swim,' she said. 'I'll have to wear armbands.'

'Lots of people wear armbands,' said Allie.

'*You* don't,' said Misha, 'and I bet Lin and Bina and Jackie-Louise don't either. I'll be with the babies.' And Misha pulled a face at herself in the mirror. It was a funny face, but Allie knew Misha didn't really think it was funny, wearing armbands and not being able to swim.

'I like your swimsuit,' said Allie. She wanted to ask, 'Do you like mine?' but she didn't. She could tell that Misha wasn't really thinking about swimsuits. She was thinking about deep swimming-pools, and having to get in quickly so nobody would think she was a baby. School swimming was going to be the very first time Misha had ever been in the swimming-pool. Everybody else was used to it. Allie wished she could think of something. Then Mum came in to see what was going on.

'You both look very nice,' she said. 'Move your arms around to make sure the straps aren't too tight, Allie.'

Allie did breast-stroke with her arms. The swimsuit felt perfect. She couldn't wait to wear it in the swimming-pool. Misha was peering at the label on her swimsuit. 'Have I got enough money for this one?' she asked Mum.

'Yes, I'll put the change in an envelope for you,' said Mum. She smiled at Misha. 'That red really suits you.'

'Mum!' Allie burst out. 'Tomorrow morning, can Misha come swimming with us?'

'Yes, all right,' said Mum, but Misha fiddled with the strap of her swimsuit and said, 'I've got to look after Vivi for Mum while she cooks dinner.'

'Please, Misha, please. If we go early, we can be the first in the pool.' Allie wanted to say to Misha, 'Don't worry. There won't be anybody from school,' but she couldn't say it with Mum there. Misha would like the swimming-pool when it was quiet and empty, early on Sunday morning, with nobody splashing and shouting, and nobody watching. Misha could get used to the pool, and then it would be easy on school swimming day.

'Maybe,' said Misha slowly.

Allie was just going into her cubicle to get changed when she heard Misha ask Mum, 'Can you buy a pair of armbands for me as well?'

'Of course,' said Mum.

Misha, Allie and Mum were first at the swimming-pool on Sunday morning. Jacqueline didn't want to come because it was so early. Allie got changed like lightning. There was the pool, still and blue and unbroken. There was Mum, tying up her hair. There was Misha, in her red swimsuit. Other people were coming now, but they weren't changed yet.

'First in!' yelled Allie, and she jumped off the side, straight into the water. There was a huge splash, and water rocked up the sides of the pool. Allie  came up through a cloud of bubbles and saw Misha. Misha had stepped back from the side of the pool. She was trying to get her armbands on, but they were stuck. She was frowning and looking down, as if she wasn't enjoying it at all. Allie felt terrible.

She wished she hadn't jumped into the pool. She hadn't even thought of helping Misha first.

Allie climbed up the steps, and went over to Misha.

'I'll wet them for you, then they'll slide on,' she said. 'Mum used to do that with my armbands.' She dipped the armbands in the pool, and helped Misha to slide them on.

'That's it,' said Allie. 'They look fine.'

'Do they?' asked Misha. She made another funny face, but it wobbled a bit. Mum was swimming with long, steady strokes, all the way down the pool.

I've got to help Misha, thought Allie. But what was the best way?

'Let's go in down the steps,' said Allie. 'If you go down backwards, you can hold on to the rails and feel each step with your feet.'

'Allie,' said Misha, 'can you go in first and stand up so I can see how deep it is?'

Allie went down the steps until she was standing in the shallow end of the pool.

'You'll be able to stand up easily,' she said to Misha.

Misha grasped the rails at the top of the steps.

'Turn round! It's much easier backwards!' called Allie.

Misha put her foot on the first step. Water lapped round it, and Allie saw how Misha's foot flinched. Then, slowly, Misha put her other foot down, on the second

30

step. The water lapped round her leg. A boy was waiting behind Misha. Allie opened her mouth to say, 'Hurry up, Misha!' Then she shut it again. She could see how strange the water felt on Misha's skin. Misha hesitated, then went down the next step. The water rose. Soon Misha's swimsuit would get wet for the first time.

'Allie! I can't feel the next step!' said Misha.

'There isn't one. You're on the bottom step. Now, reach your foot down and it'll touch the bottom of the pool.' But Misha clung tight to the rails.

'I can't feel it!'

Allie suddenly saw how much Misha wanted to shrink back up the steps. But she knew that Misha would never let herself do that. Anyway, the boy was starting to come down behind Misha. Allie held out her hands.

'I'll stand here. When you step down, you just hold on to me.'

Misha reached out one hand, and Allie grasped it. Then she reached out the other. Misha closed her eyes, and stepped off the bottom step.

'There!' said Allie. 'That's fantastic! You see, you can easily stand up.'

Misha opened her eyes and looked round. She blinked as the boy flopped off the steps. The water swayed round Misha's shoulders.

'You can't sink,' said Allie. 'The armbands won't let you.'

Misha let go of one of Allie's hands. She patted the surface of the water.

'Do you want to walk round a bit?' asked Allie. There were more people now. A father threw a baby up in the air, then caught him. Serious swimmers, like Mum, went up and down, up and down.

'I think I'll just stand here for a minute,' said Misha. She trailed her hand through the water again. 'It's quite friendly, really, isn't it?'

'What?'

'The water.'

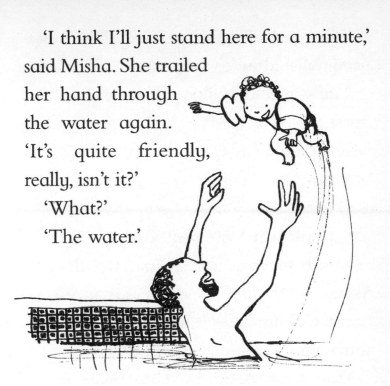

Allie thought that was a funny thing for Misha to say. But if you'd never been in it before, the huge blue surface of the pool might look unfriendly – big and cold and dangerous, covered with sharp ripples.

'At least I'll know how to get into the pool when we go swimming with school on Tuesday,' said Misha. She moved a little away from Allie. She let go of Allie's other hand. Misha took a few steps, balancing carefully and dabbling her hands in the water.

'It's great, isn't it?' said Allie.

'Hmm,' said Misha. 'It's all right. I'll get used to it.'

'I think the swimming-pool is my favourite place in the whole world,' said Allie.

'It's OK for *you*,' said Misha, 'look at your mum. My mum and dad can't swim.'

'Can't swim!' said Allie, much more loudly than she meant to say it.

'No,' said Misha. 'That's why they don't take me. There wasn't a swimming-pool anywhere near where they grew up.' Misha walked a few steps more. She turned to Allie and smiled. 'Do you know,' she said, 'the water lifts you up, doesn't it? My feet nearly came off the bottom then.'

Allie lay back in the water. She floated,

sculling a bit with her hands. She could
hear the noise of water in her ears, and she
could see Misha's face looking down on
her. Allie stood up again.

'With your armbands on, you don't even
need to learn to float,' she said. 'They'll
hold you up.'

'You mean I could do that?'

'Yes,' said Allie.

'You hold my head,' said Misha.

Misha shut her mouth tight. Allie put her
hands behind Misha's head. Slowly, slowly,
Misha's feet rose up from the bottom of the
pool. She spread out her arms and the
armbands held her up. And then Misha
was lying on her back, floating, just like

Allie had done. Allie kept her hands under Misha's head, just in case. Then slowly, slowly, Misha stood up again.

'That was very good, Misha,' said Mum, who had swum up behind them. 'I think you're going to learn to swim easily.'

Misha smiled. 'When I can swim,' she said, 'do you know what I'm going to do?'

'No, what?' asked Allie.

'I'm going to take Vivi swimming. I'm going to teach her to swim so that when she goes to school swimming she'll be as good as you.'

'I'll tell you something,' said Allie.

'What?'

'Lin wears armbands.'

'What! *Lin wears armbands!* Why didn't you tell me?'

'Why do you think?' asked Allie, and she ducked under water before Misha could splash her.

3

The big snow

Allie woke up. Jacqueline was still curled in her bed, fast asleep. Allie looked at her watch. Seven-thirteen. Friday morning.

Gym today, thought Allie, and I might finish my clay model. But something was different. The room was very light, even though it was winter. Allie sat up in bed. Something was missing. What was it? Allie heard Mum plug in the kettle downstairs. It made a loud click in the silence. Why was everything so quiet?

'No cars!' said Allie. She said it out loud by mistake, and Jacqueline groaned and turned over in bed. *No cars*. No noise of buses, or lorries, or motorbikes. Allie couldn't hear any traffic at all. But there was a tingle in the air, as if something exciting and mysterious was happening. Allie pulled the curtains open and looked out.

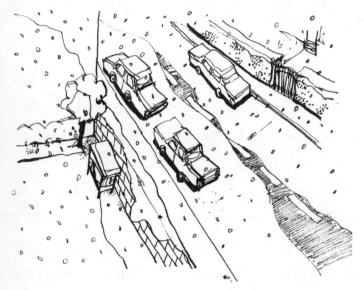

Snow! Snow everywhere. Snow thick on the white roofs, and on the white tops of cars, and on the white yard, and in the white road. The sky was greyish-yellow, full of snow. Allie looked up and saw the snowflakes falling, so thick and white and fast that it looked as if the sky had turned to snow as well.

'Jacqueline!' shouted Allie. 'Jacqueline! It's snowing!'

Nothing happened. Then a scratchy voice said from under Jacqueline's duvet, 'What? Where? Wosstime?'

'Snow!' yelled Allie. 'Snow! Snow! Snow!'

Allie loved snow. Every night in winter she watched the weather forecast and saw snow falling on the Scottish mountains. 'It's not fair, they get it all,' she said. Mum said they were welcome to it.

There was a creak of bedsprings and an earthquake of duvet. Jacqueline sprang out of bed.

'Wow!' she said. 'I'm going to phone Yasmin this minute! She's got a sledge. We'll go sledging in the park.'

'It's school today,' said Allie.

'School!' said Jacqueline. 'I don't think so.'

'Really?' asked Allie. 'Do you really

think there won't be any school today, Jacqueline?' But Jacqueline was already downstairs. Allie ran down after her. There was Mum, digging through the junk in the cupboard under the stairs.

'Get dressed *quick*, Allie,' she said. 'I've got to listen to the radio to hear if your school is open. And I can't find your boots anywhere.'

'Oh wow!' said Allie to herself as she raced upstairs to get dressed, 'Wow, wow, wow.'

'And put on something *warm*. Your red jumper!' shouted Mum up the stairs. Allie washed and dressed, put on two pairs of socks and prayed that her school would be closed. She ran back down the stairs.

'Ssh!' said Mum. A man's voice was reading a list of schools on the radio.

'The following schools are closed: Upton Junior School, Landsgrove Primary, City Hall College, Hurley Park Primary . . .'

'Hurley Park Primary!' shouted Allie and Jacqueline together. Allie was so excited that she grabbed Jacqueline's hands and jumped up and down. 'School's closed! School's closed!'

'Oh no,' said Mum. 'What am I going to do with you two? I've got to leave for work in fifteen minutes.'

'Maybe your hospital will be closed, too,' said Allie.

'No,' said Mum. 'We can't close. There won't be any buses, but I can walk to work. But what am I going to do with you two?'

'I can look after us,' said Jacqueline.

Mum looked at Jacqueline. It was a long look. Then she turned to Allie. 'You'll have to be very sensible, Allie.'

Allie wasn't sure that she would like being looked after by Jacqueline for a whole long day. Sometimes, after school, Allie stayed in the yard with Silver because Jacqueline always chose what programme they could watch on TV.

'Mum,' she said. Then she stopped. Mum *had* to go to work. The people in hospital had to have nurses to look after them, even when it was snowing. And Mum's face looked so worried.

'We'll be fine, Mum,' she said.

'We'll go sledging in the park,' said Jacqueline. 'We can go round to Yasmin's and then we'll take her sledge and some plastic bags to slide down the slope and –'

'No,' said Mum. 'I'm sorry. But you can't go to the park while I'm at work. You can play in the yard. You can go down to Mrs Patel's for sweets. You can get fish and chips at dinner-time. But no park. Promise, Jacqueline?'

'Can't I even go round to Misha's?' asked Allie.

'No. I want you to stay together, at home. It's only for one day. Tomorrow's Saturday and you can go sledging then.'

'But the snow might have gone by tomorrow!'

'Allie. Jacqueline. I'm going to be late. Now promise you'll be sensible, just for one day. Jacqueline, here's the money for fish and chips. I'll phone you from work.'

Mum leaned down to kiss them. She looked so worried that Allie swung her arms tight round Mum's neck, and hugged

her as hard as she could.

'We'll be good. I promise,' she said.

'I'll tell Mrs Patel that you two are on your own. She'll keep an eye on you. I'll give her my phone number at work,' said Mum.

'You don't need to do that. I'll look after Allie all right,' said Jacqueline. Her voice sounded different, not bossy at all. Almost grown-up, thought Allie.

The house was very quiet after Mum had gone. The snow fell faster than ever. Allie had a strange feeling inside, as if she was waiting for something to happen. But she couldn't think what it was.

'Let's go outside,' said Jacqueline. 'Mum's put your boots in the kitchen.'

'I've got to feed Silver,' said Allie. 'He's never seen snow before. He'll be so surprised.'

Allie lifted the thick blanket off Silver's hutch and opened his bedroom door. He was curled up deep in the hay but, as soon as he saw Allie, his nose twitched and his whiskers quivered.

'Come and see something you've never seen before, Silver,' said Allie. 'It's called snow.' She picked him up and stroked his long ears. He did not try to jump down on to the ground. His big toffee-coloured eyes looked astonished. Flakes of snow fell on his nose and he sneezed.

'It's cold, Silver. You wouldn't like to play in it,' said Allie.

She put him back in his hutch, and gave him carrots and rabbit food. Jacqueline had got the broom and she was sweeping a path from the back door to the gate. But the snow fell so fast that the path was covered with white again by the time Jacqueline had finished.

'We could make a snowman,' said Allie. 'I've never made a snowman.'

'Yes, you have,' said Jacqueline. 'Don't you remember?'

'No,' said Allie.

'You took the carrot out of the snowman and ate it,' said Jacqueline. 'It was meant to be his nose.'

'It must have been a long time ago,' said Allie. 'I know! We could make a snow rabbit.'

'You can if you want,' said Jacqueline in her old, bossy voice. '*I'm* going to make a proper snowman.'

Allie watched Jacqueline. She seemed to

46

know just what to do. She rolled a
snowball round the yard until it was big
enough to be a body. She rolled another
smaller snowball for the head. Then she
stuck the head to the body with lots of
snow. Allie wondered how to start making
a snow rabbit. Perhaps it would be easier
to make a lying down rabbit. Allie started
to roll a snowball, like Jacqueline. It didn't
look like a rabbit's body.

'What's that?' asked Jacqueline.

'It's part of a snow rabbit.'

'Which part?'

'Um . . . the back,' said Allie.

'It doesn't look like a rabbit to me,' said Jacqueline.

Allie put more snow 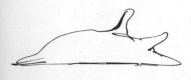 on the rabbit. She shaped two ears for it, but they fell off. She tried to make snow whiskers. But her rabbit still did not look like a rabbit. 'Please, Jacqueline, can you help me with my rabbit's face?'

'I've got to finish my snowman,' said Jacqueline.

Suddenly there was a ring at the door.

'Who's that?'

'We'd better go and look.'

They peered through the glass panel of the front door. All they could see was a big umbrella.

'It's me! Open the door. It's Mrs Patel.' Mrs Patel was wearing a thick coat over her sari. She shook the snow off her umbrella and followed Allie and Jacqueline indoors.

'I told your mother I would call to see how you are,' she explained.

'But what about the shop?' asked Allie.

'No problem, my daughter is 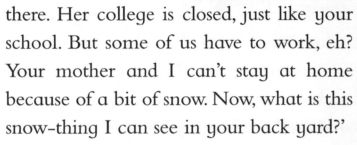 there. Her college is closed, just like your school. But some of us have to work, eh? Your mother and I can't stay at home because of a bit of snow. Now, what is this snow-thing I can see in your back yard?'

'It's a snowman!'

'It's a snow rabbit!'

'Hmm. I will come outside and look,' said Mrs Patel. She put her umbrella up again and stepped out of the back door.

'I can't make his head right,' said Allie.

'I can see what is wrong,' said Mrs Patel. 'Hold my umbrella, Jacqueline.'

Jacqueline held the umbrella high to keep the snow off Mrs Patel. Mrs Patel tucked her thick coat under her knees, and then she kneeled down by Allie's snow rabbit. She gathered the snow together and began to pat it into shape. Her hands moved quickly, slapping and shaping the snow as if it was pastry dough. The rabbit's body grew smooth and round. There was his head, with the ears laid back as if the rabbit was ready to run. There were his big, surprised-looking eyes.

'He's just like
Silver!' said Allie.

'There,' said Mrs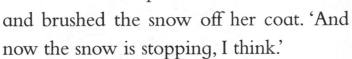
Patel. She stood up
and brushed the snow off her coat. 'And
now the snow is stopping, I think.'

Allie looked up at the sky. It was not so
grey and heavy now. It was brighter, as if
somewhere the sun was waiting to come
out. The snow rabbit crouched on the
ground, ready to run. Mrs Patel was
looking at Jacqueline's snowman.

'That is very nice, Jacqueline,' she said.
'You don't need any help. All you need is a
carrot for his nose.'

'And I won't eat it this time,' said Allie.

'Oh no,' said Mrs Patel. 'But it is cold out
here. I told your mother I would make a
hot drink for you.'

Mrs Patel made two big mugs of
steaming hot chocolate. She gave Allie and
Jacqueline a chocolate mini-roll each,

from her pocket. She wrote her phone number down on a piece of paper and gave it to Jacqueline.

'Any problem, you ring me, Jacqueline,' she said. 'We don't want to bother your mother at the hospital. When she comes home I will tell her how well you are doing.' Then Mrs Patel had to go back to the shop.

Allie drank some of her hot chocolate. It was sweet and delicious. She could see the snow rabbit through the window, and the snowman. The sky was turning blue, and the snow shone.

'Perhaps my snow rabbit will come to

life at night,' thought Allie, though she knew he wouldn't really.

'Allie!' said Jacqueline. 'I've asked you three times!'

'What?'

'Which video do you want to watch?'

Allie stared at Jacqueline. Jacqueline always chose which video they watched.

'Can I really choose, Jacqueline?'

'Oh wake up, Allie! I've just said you can.'

The video started, but Allie wasn't really watching. The hot chocolate made her sleepy. It was nice being at home with Jacqueline, when Jacqueline wasn't being bossy. Maybe Mrs Patel would come round again later and make another animal out of snow. A cat, or a hedgehog with prickly spines sticking out of his snow body. It would be easy to collect twigs to make the spines. Allie yawned and put her empty mug on the floor. Maybe it was the snow that was making her so sleepy. She had never seen so much snow. All over the yard, all over the roads, all over the houses. So deep and white that the cars and buses couldn't move.

Tomorrow they would go to the park. Yasmin and Jacqueline might let her have a go on the sledge. Or else Allie and Misha could make a really huge snowman, the biggest in the whole park. And maybe school would still be closed on Monday.

Allie shut her eyes. In her mind she could see the snow falling again. Thick, white flakes scurried out of the sky, faster and faster. Allie watched them falling and falling and — Allie was asleep.

4

The best party ever

Allie was late, late, late. Late again.

'It's your fault, Silver,' she muttered as she raced down the empty corridor. Everybody was in the classrooms already. She must have been watching Silver for ages. First of all he had nibbled his carrot right down to Allie's fingers. She loved the way his nose and whiskers quivered. And then, just when Allie was going to go, Silver had started to clean his ears with his paws. Jacqueline was shouting, 'If you don't come this *minute* I'm going without you!' but Allie just *had* to say goodbye to Silver properly.

Misha's peg was empty. That meant she was still at home with tonsillitis. Allie hung up her jacket slowly. She didn't want to go into the classroom. It was too late, too quiet, and there was no Misha to smile at her after Mrs Button had finished being cross.

Allie slid round the classroom door. Mrs Button stopped talking and looked at her.

'Oh, Allie! Late again,' she said. Somebody laughed. Everybody looked at Allie as she walked to her table. She kept her head down so no one would see how red her face was. That was why she fell over Michael Duncan's schoolbag. All his stuff shot out over the floor.

'Why can't you look where you're going?' growled Michael, picking up his felt-tips.

'I'm sorry, Michael,' said Allie, and she slipped into her chair.

'Lin, will you *please* put those party invitations away, for the last time!' said Mrs Button. Now she sounded really cross.

'You can give them out at playtime, but don't let me see them again till then.'

Allie looked sideways to where Lin was sitting with Jackie-Louise and Bina. Lin had a pile of coloured envelopes in front of her. Pink and blue and yellow and orange and red. Lin gathered up the envelopes, but she didn't do it quickly, even though Mrs Button was waiting.

'Lin! Put those envelopes in your drawer NOW,' said Mrs Button. Lin got up with the fat pile of invitations. How many were there? Ten? Fifteen? Twenty? Perhaps Lin really *was* going to invite everyone in the class to her party. Lin had been talking about it all week. It was going to be the biggest, best party ever. There was going to be a roller-disco at the sports centre, then tea at Pete's Pizza with an enormous birthday cake.

'Mum says I can't tell *anyone* what kind of cake I'm having until the party. It's a

58

surprise. And everyone's going to get *loads* of things in their party bags.'

Allie knew all about the party. Everyone did. In the playground everyone hung round Lin, hoping they were going to get an invitation. But Lin wouldn't say who was coming.

'I'm bringing in the invitations on Friday.'

And now it was Friday. Lin's glance swept round the classroom. Once she was sure everyone was looking at her, she put the envelopes in her drawer.

'Right. We'll have ten minutes' quiet reading, to give everyone time to settle down,' said Mrs Button. Allie got out her reading-book, but she couldn't think about the story. She kept thinking about Lin's party. Was Lin still her friend, just a little bit? If Lin was asking the whole class, she wouldn't leave Allie out, would she? Allie wished she could ask Misha. Misha always made things sound better.

At last it was playtime. Allie put her work away very slowly. She saw Lin go to the drawer. Allie didn't want to look any more. She didn't want to see Lin handing out her party invitations.

I'll go straight into the playground. I'll play with Sarah or Hannah. I won't even look at Lin, thought Allie.

But then Allie saw that Lin, Jackie-Louise and Bina were standing by the classroom door. Lin and Jackie-Louise on one side, Bina on the other. You had to walk past them to get out of the classroom. And Lin was holding the pile of envelopes in her hand. She was giving out her party invitations.

'Come along, Allie, outside in the fresh

air,' said Mrs Button.

Allie walked to the classroom door. She didn't look at Lin, or Jackie-Louise, or Bina. Her heart beat so hard that she could feel it knocking inside her and her hands were hot. And then, just as Allie was going through the door, Lin said, 'Wait a minute, Allie. I've got something for you.'

Allie couldn't believe it. She stared at Lin. There was a little smile on Lin's mouth as she riffled through the pile of envelopes, looking for the right one.

She's asking me to her party! thought Allie. She still couldn't believe it. But there was the envelope, in Lin's hand. A

beautiful, bright red envelope, Allie's favourite colour.

'Thank you, Lin,' said Allie.

'Can you give that to Misha for me?' said Lin. Her little smile grew bigger. 'I know you'll see her at the weekend.'

Allie looked down at the envelope. It didn't say *Allie* on it. It said *Misha*, in Lin's best curly handwriting, with a little circle over the 'i'. Allie looked down, then up again.

'Yes,' she said, but her voice didn't sound right. Lin was still smiling, and Jackie-Louise was smiling too, but Bina wasn't. Bina looked embarrassed.

'Don't huddle in the doorway, girls! Go on out to the playground,' called Mrs Button.

Allie ran. She didn't see where she was

running. Faces looked blurred. She ran right to the end of the playground, where she sometimes sat and talked with Misha when they didn't want to play with the others.

The bright red envelope was still in her hand. The playground noise echoed in Allie's head like a TV in the next room. She closed her eyes. Suddenly she heard someone calling her name. 'Allie! Allie!' It was Sarah.

'What?' said Allie.

'Do you want to play Bulldog?'

'No,' said Allie. 'I don't feel well.'

'Shall I take you to Mrs Button?'

But Allie shook her head. She knew if she went to see Mrs Button she would start

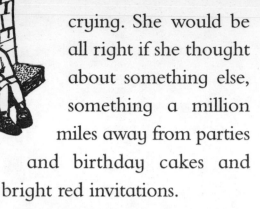

crying. She would be all right if she thought about something else, something a million miles away from parties and birthday cakes and bright red invitations.

It was the longest playtime of Allie's whole life. It was the longest day of Allie's whole life. *Everyone* had an envelope, except Allie. Everyone was opening their invitations and asking Lin about the party. Lin stood in the middle like a queen, and smiled and smiled.

On Saturday morning, Misha's Mum said Allie could come round. Misha was nearly better. She would be able to go to school on Monday. Allie took the bright red envelope out of her pocket.

'What's this?' asked Misha.

'Open it and see,' said Allie.

Misha tore open the envelope. She read the invitation carefully.

'It's an invitation to Lin's party,' she said. She sounded puzzled.

'I know,' said Allie.

'Have you got one?'

'No.'

Misha thought for a while. 'I don't know why she's asked me to her party. She doesn't even like me.'

'She's asked everyone. It's going to be the biggest party ever.'

'But she hasn't asked you,' said Misha slowly.

'No,' said Allie. It was all right when Misha said it. It didn't sound so bad.

Then Misha smiled. 'I know why she's asked me,' she said.

'Why?'

'Because she hasn't asked you.'

Allie didn't understand. Misha went on, 'She hasn't asked me because she wants *me.* She's asked me because she wants to be horrible to *you.*'

'Oh,' said Allie.

'Well, we already knew she was horrible,' said Misha. She got up and opened a drawer under the worktop and fetched a pen. Then she spread out the invitation. '*Thank you for the invitation. I shall/shall not be able to come*', it said. Carefully, Misha put a black pen line through '*shall*'.

'Aren't you going to her party?' asked Allie.

'I don't think so,' said Misha. She grinned at Allie. 'She can keep the biggest party in the world.'

'But everyone else in our class will be going.'

'I bet they won't. Did she really have thirty-two invitations?'

Allie thought. It had been a big pile of envelopes.

'Did Sarah get one? Or Hannah? Or Sushila?'

Allie tried to remember. 'I'm not sure,' she said slowly.

'Her mum would never let her ask the whole class,' said Misha confidently. 'Listen, I've got a plan.'

On Monday Lin was still talking about her party. 'Only five days to go!' she said loudly, looking round to make sure everyone was listening. The party was on Saturday afternoon. Quietly, Misha went round the classroom. When the bell rang she sat down and whispered to Allie.

'Loads of people didn't get invitations. Hannah didn't, Sushila didn't, Sarah didn't, nor did Chanelle or Claire. And hardly any of the boys got one.'

'I thought everyone had one, except me,' said Allie.

'So we can go ahead with our plan,' said Misha. 'I asked my dad last night and he said it was all right.'

At playtime Misha and Allie went quietly from one person to another. They spoke to everyone who wasn't going to Lin's party. One by one, they left what they were doing and came to the end of the playground. There were seventeen.

'There are more people not going than going,' said Sushila, and she smiled.

'Allie and I thought it would be good to have a different party, for everyone

 who isn't going to Lin's,' said Misha. 'We could have a party in the park. My dad says it's OK. He'll help us take the things up there.'

'What things?' asked Hannah.

'Food,' said Misha. 'And drinks, and balloons, and sweets, and games.'

'We could play football,' said Michael Duncan.

Jaswinder had a game of tennis on a pole, with two bats. Hannah had a cricket set. Luke had model boats to race on the park pool. Sushila had a pair of stilts and a pogo stick. Chanelle had two kites.

'I can bring crisps.'

'My dad will let us have Coke from his shop.'

'My mum will make a cake,' said Allie. Her mum was brilliant at cakes.

Misha had a piece of paper and a pencil. She wrote down what everyone was bringing.

balloons   marshmallows
sweets   popcorn
chocolate   orange squash
biscuits

'What time does the party begin?' asked Justin.

There was so much to decide.

'My mum won't let me go on my own,' said Hannah.

'Nor will mine,' said lots of other people.

'But Misha's dad will be there.'

'My dad'll come too, if I ask him,' said Michael suddenly. 'He always plays football in the park with me on Saturday afternoons.'

'It's going to be fantastic!' said Allie.

Now she didn't care if Lin had a hundred bright red envelopes. The party in the park was going to be the best party ever.

Mum and Allie worked on the cake all Saturday morning. Even Jacqueline helped. It was a big, round sponge cake with blue icing and a big, yellow-icing sunflower in the middle. Allie and Jacqueline took turns with the icing kit. Allie did the sunflower petals, then Jacqueline did the stem and the leaves in green icing.

'Now, have I got a big enough cake tin?' asked Mum.

Very slowly and carefully, she fitted the cake into her biggest round tin. There was just enough room for it.

'I'm going to lie down and rest this afternoon,' said Allie's mum.

'Oh, Mum, aren't you going to come? It's going to be the best party ever,' said Allie.

'Well, maybe,' said Mum.

Misha and Allie were at the park by quarter to three. Misha's Dad helped them carry the cake, the crisps and chocolate fingers, the iced gems and plastic cups and paper towels. Allie and Misha spread the food out on the grass under a tree.

'What if nobody comes?' said Allie.

'There's Hannah and Sarah! Look, Michael's come with Jaswinder and Luke!'

And the party began. It wasn't like an ordinary party at all. There weren't any grown ups organising things. Misha's dad lay in the sun talking to Michael's dad about football. Sushila's mum came with some sweets in a white cardboard box, but she went away again. Wherever you looked, there was something happening. There was a football game, and Jaswinder's tennis ball whizzing through the air on its elastic. Sarah on stilts raced Justin on the pogo stick. The kites nearly got caught up in the tops of the trees, and the model boats sailed right across the pond, past a family of angry ducks.

There was so much food Allie didn't think it would ever get eaten. Biscuits and crisps and sweets and sausages on sticks and popcorn and chocolate rolls. Everybody had brought something. And the cake. The best cake Mum had ever made. Allie hoped Mum would come up to the park to see it before it got eaten.

Misha flopped down on the grass beside Allie. She was out of breath from racing.

'Do you think it's time for tea yet?' she asked Allie.

'I'm hungry,' said Allie. 'Isn't it a fantastic party?'

'Mmm,' said Misha. 'Listen, Allie, you'll have to thank Lin on Monday.'

'*Thank Lin*? What do you mean? She didn't ask me to her party!'

'I know. But that's why we're having this party. That's why you ought to thank her!'

'I will!' said Allie. 'I'll thank her. I'll say, "Thank you for making us have the best party in the world." '

'You won't,' said Misha.

'Why won't I?'

'Because you're not horrible.' Misha smiled and rolled over on her back and shut her eyes.

It was nearly time to eat. Allie could hear all her friends, shouting and calling and laughing. She could see the pile of food. And in the middle there was the big cake Mum had made. The best cake ever. The best party ever. The yellow sunflower shone in the blue sky on top of the cake.